ALL HE

www.realreads.co.uk

Retold by Tony Evans
Illustrated by Sarah Wimperis

Published by R_____ Ltd

_____d, Glouce_____shire, UK

www.r_____.uk

Text copyright © Tony Evans 2013
Illustrations copyright © Sarah Wimperis 2013
The right of Tony Evans to be identified as author of
this book has been asserted by him in accordance with the
Copyright, Design and Patents Act 1988

First published in 2013

ISBN 978-1-906230-66-1

Printed in China by Wai Man Book Binding (China) Ltd
Designed by Lucy Guenot
Typeset by Bookcraft Ltd, Stroud, Gloucestershire

CONTENTS

THE CHARACTERS

Paul Bäumer

Paul is only nineteen years old and has left school to join the army. He has never been away from home before. How will he cope with life in the trenches?

Fredrich Müller

Fredrich is one of Paul's old schoolmates. He loves to study and wants to take his exams after the war. Will he survive the horrors of the battlefield?

Albert Kropp

Another young man who was at school with Paul, Albert is the cleverest of them all. But will his intelligence help him when he is sent to the front line?

Stanislaus Katczinsky

Katczinsky, known as Kat, is old enough to be Paul's father. He is very good at finding food and shelter, and the young soldiers admire him. Can he help them to deal with the hardships of war?

Tjaden

Tjaden was a locksmith before the war, and is only nineteen. He loves his food but never seems to put on weight.

Paul's mother

Paul's mother has been unwell for some time, but she has not told her son. How will he feel when he returns home on leave and finds her ill in bed?

Kantorek

Kantorek was Paul's teacher before the war, and persuaded Paul and his classmates to join the army. What will happen when he joins the Home Defence Force and finds that one of his old pupils is in charge?

ALL QUIET ON THE WESTERN FRONT

We are nine kilometres behind the front line.
For the last two weeks we have been in the
trenches, facing the enemy, but now it's our
turn to get a few days' rest.

We've all had as much beef and beans to
eat as we wanted, and we are feeling satisfied
and happy. In fact there's such a lot of food that
the cook has been giving out extra portions.
Tjaden and Müller have even filled up a couple
of washing bowls. Müller wants to make sure
he has some food for later, if he needs it –
Tjaden is just greedy.

All this extra grub wasn't good news for
everyone. There were a hundred and fifty men
in our company when we went up into the
front line, and because it was pretty quiet in
our stretch of the trenches, the quartermaster
ordered enough supplies for the lot of us.

Then on the last day the British heavy guns shelled us from long range. High explosives landed all over our positions, and only eighty of us got back. The rest were either killed or injured. So we've had almost double rations – not just the beans and beef, but extra sausage, bread and tobacco.

I look at my comrades who are sitting in the camp hut, making the most of their break from the fighting. Four of us are nineteen years old, and last year we came straight out of the same class at school to join the army.

Nearest to me is little Albert Kropp, the cleverest pupil, who was the first to be promoted to lance-corporal. Next there's Müller, who wants to take his exams after the war, and still carries his school books around. Then Leer, who has grown a beard. All he can think about is girls.

As for me, the last of the classmates, I'm Paul Bäumer.

Since the four of us joined up we've made some good friends amongst the other recruits. Tjaden is the same age as we are. He eats more than anyone, but somehow he stays as thin as a stick, apart from his pot-belly when he's had a good meal. Before the war he was a locksmith.

Haie Westhus is the same age too. He was a labourer – a peat-digger – and he's a big lad with huge hands.

Detering is older. He's a farmer, and married, and is always talking about his wife and his farm.

Finally there's the leader of our little group, Stanislaus Katczinsky. We all call him Kat. Kat is forty years old, tough, cunning and clever. He's got a weather-beaten face, blue eyes and bent shoulders. He's helped us a lot. He always knows where to scrounge some good food, and how to make sure that our company gets the easiest jobs.

Later I sit outside with Müller and Kropp
for a game of cards. Kropp is reading a letter
he has had from home.

'Kantorek sends his best wishes,' Kropp
said.

We laugh. Müller throws away his cigarette
end and says, 'I wish he was out here with us!'

Kantorek was our class teacher at school, a strict little man with sharp features, who was always smartly dressed. He kept on telling us that we should join the army, until in the end the whole class marched down to the local barracks and volunteered. I can still remember him pleading with us to join up, with his emotional voice and tearful eyes. It all seems false and sentimental now, but we were fooled at the time.

There was only one of us who didn't want to go to war, Joseph Behm. He was a fat, cheerful boy and in the end he was persuaded. Poor Joseph didn't last long at the front – he was one of the first of our company to be killed.

He was wounded in the eye when we attacked, and we thought he was dead. Then later that day we heard him call out, and saw him crawling about in no man's land – the ground between our trenches and the enemy's. He was blinded and couldn't see to take cover, and he was shot before anyone could rescue him.

Of course we couldn't blame Kantorek directly for Behm's death. Our teacher was just one of thousands of older people, all thinking that they were doing the right thing when they encouraged us to go and fight. We had looked up to them, until we experienced the death and destruction of war – then we knew that they were wrong. We loved our country as much as they did, so we fought bravely in every battle. But we realised that the advice and opinions of our elders was worthless. The world they believed in had gone, and we were alone.

Later that afternoon we decide to visit Franz Kemmerich, who got a bullet through the leg a few days earlier, and is in the field hospital nearby. Müller says he hopes Kemmerich's got a lucky wound – not too serious, but enough to mean he'll be sent home for the rest of the war.

The hospital is very busy, and smells of disinfectant, pus and sweat.

'How's things, Franz?' asks Kropp.

'It's not so bad ... except for that damned pain in my foot.'

We glance at each other. The nurse has already told us that Kemmerich's leg has been amputated – his foot is gone. He looks very ill, his face yellow and thin. His flesh is stretched over his forehead, and his cheekbones stick out. It's as if his skeleton is working its way through his skin.

I glance at Müller and Kropp. We know that Kemmerich hasn't got much longer to live.

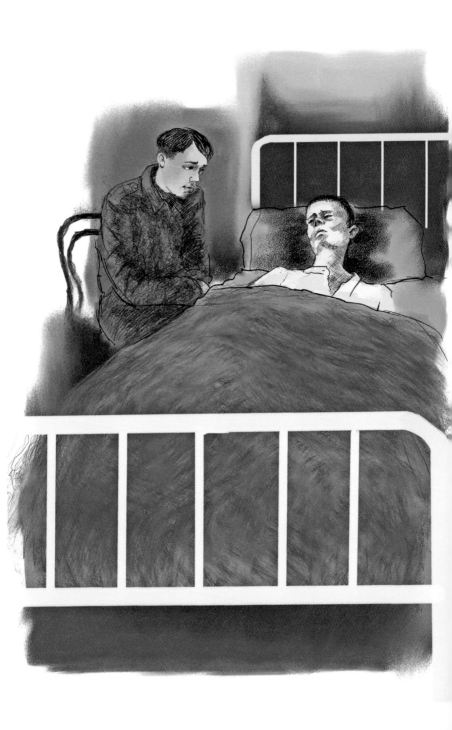

'Perhaps they'll send you to that rest home in Klosterberg,' Müller says. 'You'll be able to look out over the countryside from your window. I expect they'll have a piano, and you can play again.'

We talk for a bit longer, and promise to visit Kemmerich again soon.

The next day a message arrives from the field hospital. Kemmerich is dead.

We are ordered back to the front line on wiring duty – laying coils of barbed wire to make it more difficult for the British and French to attack. Trucks come to pick us up as soon as it starts to get dark. The engine clatters and the truck bumps along the rough track. Alongside us there are lorries loaded with shells and ammunition, in a hurry to overtake. We shout and joke with the drivers. We pass a group of our own heavy artillery, and they fire just behind us.

The flash from the guns shoots through the mist, and now we can hear the British guns reply, to the right of our position. We shiver, and are glad that we'll be back in our huts by morning.

We reach the equipment store, close to the front line trenches, and pick up rolls of barbed wire and iron posts. The horizon glows red. Flares shoot up into the night, then drift down under little silk parachutes, lighting everything up as clear as day. The thunder of the big guns is louder now, and we can hear the chattering noise of machine-guns close by.

After we finish fixing the barbed wire we head back across a field to the place where the trucks are supposed to collect us. It's three o'clock in the morning. Katczinsky looks worried, and that is a bad sign.

'What's the matter, Kat?' Kropp asks.

'I just wish we were back at the camp.'

'It won't be long now, Kat.'

He seems nervous. 'I'm not sure, I'm not sure ... '

As he speaks there is a whistling sound behind us, shells pass overhead and explode in a sheet of flame a hundred metres away.

'Take cover!' someone shouts.

The field is flat and the only place for us to hide is a military graveyard close by, with little mounds of earth marked by black wooden crosses. We run towards it and soon every man is lying flat behind one of the graves.

It's not a moment too soon. Shells land all around us and the flashes of the explosions light up the cemetery. Not far away someone has been hit, and I can hear screaming. Great lumps of earth come raining down upon us. I wipe the mud out of my eyes. A hole has been blown in the ground right in front of me, and I manage to crawl into it.

I tell myself that shells don't often land in the same place twice. A few moments later Kat and Kropp join me – they must have had the same idea.

In between the noise of the exploding shells we hear a bell ringing, and the sound of metal rattles. It's a warning – the enemy are using gas!

In a panic I tear my gas-mask out of its case and shove it over my head. Is it airtight? I remember the horrible scenes in the field hospital, when soldiers who had been gassed had been brought in. They'd cough and choke for days, spitting out pieces of their burned lungs.

My head is throbbing inside the gas mask as I breathe in the stale air. A second round of shellfire bursts all around us. We settle down to wait until dawn.

The shelling has stopped, and in the grey light of morning I see a man standing without his gas mask. I rip my mask off, and the fresh air streams into my lungs like cold water.

The graveyard is wrecked. There are open coffins and corpses all round us. It's as if they've been killed twice over – the second time to save us.

Kropp comes across a wounded soldier, a young recruit. Kat starts to cut off the man's uniform, and we see that his hip joint has been smashed to bits. It's a real mess of blood and bone. Before long the poor fellow will be screaming in agony.

Kat looks round and whispers. 'He's going to die anyway. Shouldn't we just shoot him, and put an end to his suffering?'

I nod, but then some more soldiers arrive, so we go off to find a stretcher.

'Poor lad,' Kat says. 'He's just a kid … '

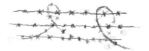

Müller and Kropp are arguing about the war. Kropp has a theory. He thinks that all declarations of war should be like a circus, with entrance tickets and music to entertain the audience. The top people from each country – generals, prime ministers and so on – would face each other in the ring, wearing boxing shorts. They would be given rubber truncheons so that they could fight each other. Whoever was left standing at the end, his country could be declared the winner. That would be simpler and fairer than the situation in France, where the wrong people are doing the fighting.

We all like Kropp's idea.

Tjaden comes into our hut and tells us that we are being sent back to the front line, two days earlier than planned. He's heard that the British and French are going to attack our trenches in a new offensive.

That means more danger for us, but everything out here depends on chance. A few months ago I was playing cards in a dugout, then after a while I walked across to another dugout to talk to some friends. When I got back to the first dugout, there was nothing left of it – a heavy shell had blown it to bits. So I walked back to my friends, just in time to help dig them out. Their trench had been hit just after I left. You see, every soldier has to trust his luck.

Our unit – Second Company – has been sent new recruits, and we are back to a hundred and fifty men. We're in the front line again, and for days there has been heavy shelling from the British artillery. Our dugout shakes, and the night roars and flashes. We hear the heavy, fierce thud when a shell lands close by, like a blow from the claws of some angry beast of prey.

Our position has almost gone. In many places the parapet is only half a metre high, and the trench is full of holes, craters and piles of earth.

A shell explodes in front of us, and everything goes dark. We are buried and have to dig ourselves out. After an hour the entrance is clear again, and we are a bit calmer because we have had something to take our minds off things.

How many more days and nights can we survive this madness – this fire and constant thunder? We have reached the limit of our endurance – then suddenly there are no more explosions close by. The artillery barrage has ended. Instead, we can hear our own guns opening fire on the trenches ahead of us. The enemy is advancing, and we must repel them.

It's hard to believe there are any of us left after the days of shelling, but all along our line of trenches our soldiers in steel helmets are appearing. Fifty metres from us a machine-gun has already been set up and is spitting out bullets.

The barbed wire has been badly damaged by the enemy shellfire but enough is left to slow up the enemy. We can see the soldiers coming across no man's land towards us. We recognise their helmets – they are French. Our artillery fires. Machine-guns and rifles join in. Haie and Kropp throw hand-grenades towards the advancing troops as fast as they can.

A whole line of them are mown down by the machine-gun next to us. I see one of the French soldiers caught on barbed wire, his face turned to the sky. His hands are lifted up, as if he is praying. Then his body falls away, and only the stumps of his arms and his hands – they've been shot off – are left hanging on the wire.

When more men surge across from the enemy trenches, we retreat to the next line of defence, just as we've planned. We throw hand-grenades behind us as we go. The position that we have abandoned is just a mess of craters and bits of crumbling trench.

We make it back to our reserve trenches, where fresh troops welcome us. The enemy haven't gained much ground, and their losses are worse than they expected. They try to advance further, but their attack is destroyed by our big guns, and they have to stop.

We don't get the chance to rest for long. We are ordered to counter-attack, and we scramble over the top of the trench towards the enemy. Next to me a lance-corporal has his head blown off. He runs on for a few paces with blood spouting up from his neck like a fountain, until his body hits the ground.

The enemy are driven back. We reach our old front line, and then advance beyond it, towards the French trenches. This back and forth attacking and counter-attacking is hell! When we get to our reserve trenches we just want to crawl into them and hide for a while. But no, we are ordered to turn round again into the nightmare of war.

Suddenly we reach the enemy lines. We are
close behind the retreating soldiers and we get
there almost as soon as they do, so we don't
have too many casualties. An enemy machine-
gun starts to fire, but we silence it with a hand-
grenade. Even so, in those few seconds five of
us get shot in the stomach. Kat smashes one
of the machine-gunners with his rifle butt,
and we bayonet the others. We throw more
grenades along our section of the trench, and
the fighting stops.

It's too dangerous for us to stay in the
enemy trenches for long, because soon they
will counter-attack. So we grab whatever food
we can see – tins of corned beef, butter, that
kind of thing – and return to our own lines.
We try to get the enemy's food whenever we
have the chance, because our own rations are
rubbish. Their soldiers are well looked after
compared with us.

The days pass by and attacks alternate with
counter-attacks. Slowly the dead bodies pile
up in no man's land, between our trenches
and the enemy's. We lose a lot of men, mainly
young recruits from the latest age-group to be
conscripted. They've had a bit of training,
but their knowledge about how to survive
out here is hopeless. They don't know the
difference between the sound of a big shell
which passes right over, and the whistle of a
dangerous low-flyer heading straight for them.

They flock together like frightened sheep instead of spreading out and finding some cover, and end up being blown to pieces, or machine-gunned by enemy aeroplanes.

We feel sorry for them. When they are killed, their thin, pale faces are like those of dead children. Most of them are so young that their uniforms are too big for them, and flap round their narrow shoulders. There weren't any uniforms small enough for these kids.

For every experienced soldier who is killed, we lose between five and ten of these recruits. One day a surprise gas attack finished off a lot of them. They didn't know what to do, and took their gas masks off too soon. Their faces turned blue and their lips black – those who weren't killed straight away swallowed enough gas to die later, coughing up blood and choking.

We manage to hold our ground against the enemy, and have only had to retreat a few hundred metres. But our casualties have been terrible – for every metre there is a dead man.

Haie Westhus gets a horrible wound which tears open his back. You can see his exposed lungs pulsing as he breathes. I squeeze his hand.

'That's me finished, Paul,' he groans, and he bites his arm because of the pain.

We see men still alive with the tops of their skulls missing. We see soldiers still running when both feet have been shot off – they stagger on their splintered stumps to the next shell hole.

Finally the day comes when we are relieved, and the trucks arrive to take us back to our camp well behind the front line. When the trucks stop, people call out the numbers of the battalions and companies who are to get off there. At each halt a pitifully small handful of pale, dirty soldiers climbs down.

Then it's our turn. I see Kat and Albert, so I
join them and we walk towards the group.

'Second Company, over here!'

Then more softly: 'Nobody else from
Second Company? Is that all? Right, lead off!'

A short line of us shuffle off. There were
a hundred and fifty of us when we went up to
the front, and now there are only thirty-two.

It's funny how quickly we seem to forget about the trenches, now that we are back at base again. Of course we don't really forget anything – we just put it out of our minds, because if we thought about it all the time, we'd go mad. A lot of our mates are dead – Kemmerick, Haie Westhus, Meyer, Marks, Hammerling and others – but we can't help them by worrying. At least they are at peace now. It's best that we sleep, and smoke, eat and drink as much as we can, to fill the passing hours. Life is short, so we may as well make the best of it.

I'm sent to the Company Commander. He tells me that I'm due some leave. Seventeen days all together! I realise that I'll be able to go home, and see my mother, father and sisters. After that I'm being sent to a training camp before I return to the front line.

My life before the war seems very distant. It's strange to think that at home in my desk drawer there is the first part of a play that I started to write, and a bundle of poems. I spent many evenings working on them – we all did things like that – but now it's unreal to me. When we came out here it's as if our old life was suddenly cut off. It's different for the older men, with wives, children and jobs. But us twenty-year-olds hadn't really started out on life. We didn't have much: just our parents, school, a girlfriend in some cases, and a few hobbies. Now nothing of that is left.

The next day Albert and Kat walk down with me to the railhead. We say goodbye.

'Take care, Kat; take care, Albert.'

They leave, their figures getting smaller as they walk away. I would recognise them at any distance. Then they are gone, and I sit down on my pack to wait for my train.

As the train gets closer to home, the scenery changes. I can see flat meadows, quiet fields and farmyards. A solitary team of horses stands out against the sky-line, on a path which runs parallel to the horizon. There are girls waving, children playing on the railway embankment, and no big guns anywhere.

I get out at the station, and walk along the road I have known all my life. The old bridge across the river is still there, and I remember how not long ago we used to sit there on hot days, enjoying the spray from the weir and chatting about our teachers.

When I get home the first person I meet is my eldest sister. She tells me that my mother has been ill for weeks, but did not want anyone to tell me, in case I became worried about her. The doctors think it might be cancer.

I go upstairs to see her. 'It's me, Mother. Paul. I'm home on leave.'

She looks weak and thin. 'My dear boy,' Mother says softly.

Our family has never been very emotional, and when she uses those simple words I can tell how much she cares for me. I give my mother the food I have brought back for them – cheese, bread, butter, cans of sausage and a bag of rice. We soldiers don't get fed very well, but we get more than they do at home.

Later, when my father arrives, he asks me about the war, but I don't say much. I change into civilian clothes, and he takes me to the beer garden, where all the men want to shake me by the hand and buy me a drink.

I go along with it all, but it's really impossible to describe what it's like in the trenches. Besides, I don't want to worry my mother. One old fellow thinks he knows all about it.

'You soldiers need to get a move on – there's been enough of this trench fighting. You need to smash into them, and finish off the war quick.'

I drink up my beer and leave.

After I've been home for a few days I bump into one of my school friends, Mittelstaedt. He's been wounded, and is stationed at the local barracks while he's recovering. Mittelstaedt has a great bit of news for me. Our old schoolmaster – Kantorek – has been called up into the Home Defence Force.

'I've got myself attached to his company,' Mittelstaedt says. 'I make him do drill every morning – you should see him! I've kitted him out in an old uniform that makes him look like an idiot, and I order him about just like he used to do to me back in school. I send him across town each day with a little handcart to collect the bread ration. Everyone laughs at his faded tunic and big boots.'

'Brilliant!' I say. 'But hasn't he made an official complaint?'

Mittelstaedt smiles. 'Yes, but our commanding officer roared with laughter when he heard the story. He doesn't like schoolmasters.'

The last week of my leave goes very quickly, and I can tell that my mother is counting the days I have left. That's the trouble with leave – it's so hard going back to the war, it would almost be better not to come home at all.

After I say goodbye to my family, I report to the training camp where I am to spend the next couple of weeks. Each day we practise drills out on the moor, amongst the juniper bushes. It's okay as long as you don't expect to get much out of it.

The woods with their birch trees are beautiful. Their colour changes all the time.

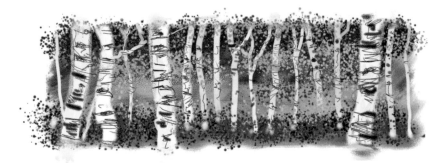

First the trunks shine a dazzling white, with pastel green leaves waving between them, then all at once it can darken almost to black when a cloud passes across the sun.

I become so fascinated by the patterns of light and shadow that I almost forget to obey the sergeant's commands. I don't know many of the other soldiers here, and when you are on your own you start to look closely at the world of nature, and to love it.

Next to our barracks there is a big prison camp for captured Russian soldiers. They are in a terrible state, very thin and always begging for food, and I feel sorry for them. It is strange to see these men – our enemies – so near to us. They have the honest faces of country folk, with broad foreheads, big hands and thick hair.

It makes you stop and think. Surely they should be out ploughing, or harvesting, or apple picking – not stuck here half-starved. Suddenly I'm scared of my own thoughts. We're at war, and that's that.

In many ways it is a relief to get back to our base again. Second Company has been in the front line, and the sergeant tells me to wait for them to get back, because they are due to return in a couple of days.

When they straggle back to base, tired, dirty and fed-up, I look for my friends. Müller is there, blowing his nose, then I spot Tjaden, Kat and little Albert Kropp. It's good to see them again. They tell me that many of our men have been killed in the recent fighting.

Later that day I give them some food which I've brought from home – potato pancakes and jam. The two on top are a bit mouldy, so I eat those myself. 'I suppose these are from your mother,' Kat says. 'They taste good.'

I could almost cry. I can hardly control my feelings. But it will be all right now I'm back with Kat and Albert and the others. This is where I belong.

After a while we talk about the war. Kropp thinks that if we're lucky we might all be sent to Russia, where the fighting has finished.

'What I'd like to know is, why is there a war at all?' asks Tjaden. 'I've got no argument with the French – most of them, they're just ordinary people, like us. Why would a French locksmith or a French shoemaker or clerk want to attack us? And the war's no good to the Kaiser either. He's the Emperor of Germany, so he's got all he needs already.'

Kat interrupts. 'That's not true. He hasn't had a war yet. And all the best emperors need at least one war, otherwise they don't get famous. Check it in your school history books!'

'Generals get famous because of wars, too,' Detering adds. 'And I bet there are other people making money out of it.'

'I think it's more like a kind of madness,' says Albert. 'No one really wants war, then all of a sudden it starts. We didn't want war, and the other side says the same – but half the world's fighting. Best not to talk about the damn business.'

Kat agrees. 'It won't change anything, anyway.'

We don't get sent to Russia – instead we are ordered back to the front line again. We've stopped counting the weeks out here. The fighting seems to be going on forever, and the war is going badly for Germany. We have no decent food, and are thin and hungry.

Fresh American troops are arriving to join the British and French. Our side is running out of men – the new recruits are pitiful, just fit to be shot down and nothing more.

One by one my little group of friends are being destroyed by the war. Sometimes people just can't take any more. Take Detering, for example. We came across a cherry tree in someone's garden, covered in white blossom. Detering told us about the big orchard full of cherry trees that he had back home, on his farm, then he went very quiet. In the morning he was gone – trying to get back to Germany. Of course this was stupid, and a week later we heard that the police had caught him. We never saw him again. I expect he was shot for desertion.

Albert Kropp has been badly wounded. He was hit by a shell splinter just above his knee, and after being patched up at a field hospital he was sent back to Germany. Later we heard that his whole leg had been amputated, from the top of his thigh downwards.

Müller is dead. He got a signal flare in the stomach at close range. He lived for half an hour after that, conscious and in terrible pain. In another attack our Company Commander, Bertinck, is killed. He survived two years without a scratch, so something had to happen in the end. The piece of shrapnel that smashes Bertinck has enough force left to tear open Leer's side. Leer bleeds to death very quickly. He was so good at maths at school, but what use is that to him now?

The months stagger on. This summer of 1918 is the bloodiest and hardest yet. Everyone knows that Germany is losing the war, but the fighting and dying continues. We hear rumours that there might be peace, but nothing happens. Why don't they stop it?

One hot and damp day in late summer Kat topples over next to me. He has been badly wounded between his knee and his ankle. His shin bone seems to be in pieces. I bandage up the leg as best I can.

'Why did that have to happen now?' Kat groans. 'Just when there's talk of the war being nearly over?'

There is no-one else around, so I decide to pick Kat up and carry him on my back to the first aid post. He isn't very heavy, and apart from a couple of rests I keep going. It is dangerous to stop still for long. Shells whistle past as I trudge onwards. Suddenly I feel afraid. Kat is the only one left of the group of soldiers who I had gone to war with almost three years ago. If he is sent home, I'll have no friends here at all.

'Kat, we must keep in touch, if peace comes before you get back,' I say.

'Do you think that leg will ever be any good?' he asks bitterly.

'The joint isn't damaged. You'll be alright, you'll see.'

Eventually I stagger into the casualty station, exhausted. I drop to my knees, my legs and hands trembling. At least Kat is safe now, I think. Then I hear someone talking to me.

'You've wasted your time,' a doctor says.

I stare at him. What can he mean?

He points to Kat. 'He's dead.'

'But it's just a leg wound.'

'Yes, that as well.' The doctor turns Kat's head to one side to show me. It must have happened when I was carrying him on my back. There is a little hole, with blood around it. A tiny fragment from an exploding shell must have pierced his skull. Private Stanislaus Katczinsky is dead.

I stand up slowly. After that I remember nothing more.

It's autumn 1918 now, and I'm the last of the little group from my school who all joined up together.

Everyone is talking about an agreement to stop fighting. I'm sure that peace will come soon. Then we can go home.

I worry about what things will be like if I am still alive after the war. All us young men, the ones who had no experience of life before they were sent off to fight, will find it hard to fit in. We don't have wives and jobs to go back to, and there's a new generation of youngsters back home now, ready to take our places.

But perhaps these thoughts of mine are too sad and gloomy. Maybe everything will be all right when I'm back home again, and there's something to look forward to.

I get to my feet, feeling very calm. I've been through so much I'm not afraid any more. If there is a life for me in the future, I will try to make the best of it.

That is the end of Paul Bäumer's story. He died in October 1918, on a day that was so peaceful and quiet along the whole front line that the army dispatch said simply: 'Nothing new to report on the Western Front'.

Paul's body was found slumped forwards, as if he was asleep on the ground. When he was turned over, you could see that he had not suffered for long. His face had a peaceful expression, almost as if he was glad that the end had come like that.

TAKING THINGS FURTHER

The real read

This *Real Reads* version of *All Quiet on the Western Front* is a retelling of Erich Maria Remarque's famous original work. If you would like to read the full story, many complete translations of this book are available, from bargain paperbacks to beautiful hardbacks. You should be able to find a copy in your local library, bookshop or charity shop. If you can read German, or if you ever decide to study the language, the original title is *Im Westen nichts Neues*.

Filling in the spaces

The loss of so many of Remarque's original words is a sad but necessary part of the shortening process. We have had to make some difficult decisions, omitting subplots and details, some important, some less so, but all interesting. We have also, at times, taken the liberty of combining two events into one, or of giving a character words or actions that originally belong to another. The points below will fill in some of the gaps, but nothing can beat the original.

- The original book begins with an epigraph – a few words written before the start of the story. This is what the epigraph says:

> *This book is neither an accusation nor a confession. It just tries to tell the story of a generation of men who were destroyed by the war – including those who survived the shelling without being killed or injured.*

- Paul describes the training camp that he and his classmates are sent to after they join up. They are bullied by Corporal Himmelstoss, an unpleasant man who tries to make their life a misery. Later Himmelstoss is sent to the front line and is eventually accepted by Paul and the other soldiers.

- When they are at base camp Paul and his comrades make friends with some French women. Paul and the others sneak out from their billets one night and swim across a canal to visit them.

- Paul visits Kemmerich's mother when he is home on leave. He says nothing about

Kemmerich's amputation or fatal illness, and tells her that her son was shot through the heart and died instantly. She does not believe him at first, but he swears that it is the truth and she eventually trusts his word.

- Paul volunteers to go out on patrol near the enemy front line. He gets cut off from the other soldiers and has to shelter in a shell hole. A French soldier falls in and Paul kills him with his knife. Paul can't stop thinking about what has happened. His friends tell him that he had no choice.

- Paul and his comrades are sent to guard a village that has been abandoned by its inhabitants. They find plenty of food and spend a couple of weeks living in great comfort.

- We are told a lot more about how Albert Kropp is wounded. Paul is also injured, but less seriously. They are both sent to a hospital in Germany, and Paul is sent back to the front line after he recovers.

Back in time

All Quiet on the Western Front was first published in book form in 1929, eleven years after the end of the First World War. Although it is a work of fiction, the events of the book are based on the author's real life experiences. Erich Maria Remarque joined the German army in 1916, when he was eighteen years old – at the same age as the main character in the story, Paul Bäumer. Remarque was sent to the front line in 1917, where he was wounded. He then spent some time in hospital and did not return to active service.

The First World War was very different from the many previous wars experienced in Europe and in the rest of the world before 1914, and came as a terrible shock to those involved. For the first time modern weapons such as machine-guns and heavy artillery firing huge explosive shells were used on a very large scale. The senior army officers on both sides had no experience of this kind of warfare, and their main tactic was to keep sending thousands of soldiers out of their trenches across open ground to try to capture the enemy trenches opposite them. The result was a dreadful loss of life. Over eight million soldiers were killed, and many millions more were seriously wounded. Large numbers of civilians also died in the conflict.

An agreement to cease fighting – the armistice – took effect on 11th November 1918. In this book Paul is killed in October 1918, so his death took place just before the First World War ended. Sadly, thousands of soldiers died in the last weeks and days of the war, just like Paul.

Remarque's war novel quickly became a best seller, and was translated into many languages. Lots of readers of the book in 1929 would have had the same experiences as Paul and his comrades, or had relatives or friends who fought in the war on one side or the other.

Finding out more

We recommend the following books and websites to gain a greater understanding of Erich Maria Remarque and the world he lived in.

Books

- Robert Graves, *Goodbye to All That*, Penguin Classics, 2000.
The author describes his experiences as a young British army officer in the First World War.

- Ruth Brocklehurst and Henry Brook, *The Usborne Introduction to the First World War*, Usborne Publishing, 2007.

- Terry Deary, *The Frightful First World War* (Horrible Histories), Scholastic, 2007.

- Jim Eldridge, *The Trenches: A First World War Soldier, 1914–1918* (My Story), Scholastic, 2008.

Websites

- www.bbc.co.uk/history/worldwars/wwone/
Includes a 'virtual tour' of the trenches.

- www.firstworldwar.com
Multimedia site which includes video and
audio clips from 1914–18.

- www.wwibattlefields.co.uk

Films

All Quiet on the Western Front (1930) directed
by Lewis Milestone. There have been more
recent screen adaptations of Remarque's book,
but none can compare with this classic film.

Food for thought

Here are a few things to think about if you are
reading *All Quiet on the Western Front* alone, or
ideas for discussion if you are reading it with
friends.

In retelling *All Quiet on the Western Front* we
have tried to recreate, as accurately as possible,

Remarque's original plot and characters. We have also tried to imitate aspects of his style. Remember, however, that this is not the original work; thinking about the points below, therefore, can help you to begin to understand Remarque's craft. To move forward from here, turn to the full-length version of *All Quiet on the Western Front* and lose yourself in his exciting and imaginative story.

Starting points

● Apart from Paul, which other character in the book do you find most interesting?

● A lot of the book is written in the present tense – for example, 'Leer looks round' rather than 'Leer looked round'. What do you think Paul's story gains from this?

● When Paul's former teacher, Kantorek, is called up to join the Home Defence Force, Paul's school friend Mittelstaedt bullies Kantorek and makes him look stupid. Why does Mittelstaedt do this? Is it right for him to pick on Kantorek?

● Why do you think that Remarque decided that his fictional character, Paul, should be killed just a few weeks before the end of the war?

● The causes of the First World War were very complicated. Many people, including soldiers who fought bravely, were not sure about the reasons for the conflict. What do Paul and his comrades seem to think about the reasons for the war?

Themes

What do you think Remarque is saying about the following themes in *All Quiet on the Western Front*?

● the horrors of trench warfare

● comradeship – Paul's close attachment to his friends

● the different attitudes to the war of those serving in the front line, and the civilians back home

● the part played by chance and fate in human affairs

Style

Can you find paragraphs containing examples of the following?

● descriptions of particularly horrific events or scenes which are intended to shock the reader

● descriptions of peaceful surroundings which contrast with the battlefield scenes

● short, plain sentences and straightforward speech which add realism and directness to the story

● descriptions of characters that help us to picture them as we read the story

Look closely at how these paragraphs are written. What do you notice? Can you write a paragraph in the same style?